Mouse Builds a House

Published by Thar She Blows Books
©2011 Tracy Sabin

Amazon print version
©2019 Tracy Sabin

ISBN 978-1-7930761-0-6

tharsheblowsbooks.com

Mouse Builds a House

TRACY SABIN

Thar She Blows Books

One day, Mouse said, "Mom, Pop, it's time I went into the wide world!"

"Waaa!" Mom cried. "I knew this day was coming!"

"But, where will you live?" Pop said.

"I will build a house," said Mouse.

"Does this mean I get your room?" his sister asked.

Mouse walked far up the river until he found the perfect spot.
"This is where I will build my house," he said.

He drew some plans.

He found reeds by the riverbank.

He snipped and stacked and tied until his house was built.

"There," he said.

"Isn't this a fine house?"

That night there was thunder and lightning. Buckets of rain poured down. Hail pounded on the roof.

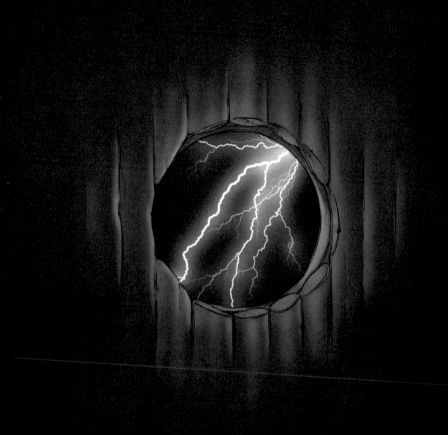

The next morning, Mouse looked at the bright, blue sky...

...from INSIDE his bedroom!

"Burripp," said Frog. "Really now, old chap. Don't you know around these parts you have to build your roof with red tiles?"

"I did not know that," said Mouse.

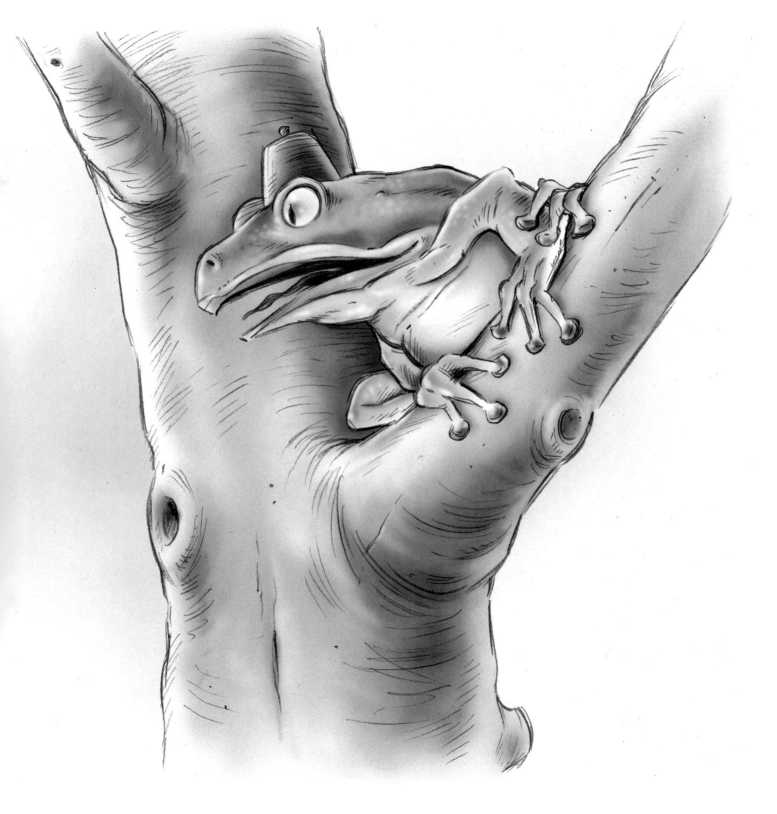

He found red clay by the river bank.
He shaped it into tiles.

He baked the tiles in an
oven until they were hard.

He placed the tiles in a neat row
on his rooftop.

"There," he said. "Isn't this a fine house?"

That night the wind blew. It howled and whistled. Whooo! Eeeee!
Branches snapped. Trees fell down.

The next morning, Mouse looked around at the calm new day...

... from INSIDE his bedroom!

"Glubbub," gurgled Turtle, paddling upriver. "Good golly, guy. Don't you know around these parts you have to build your walls out of wood?"

"I did not know that," said Mouse.

He gathered trees blown
down by the wind.

He sawed and shaped.

He hoisted and hammered until
he was done.
"There," he said. "Isn't this a
fine house?"

That night the river rose. It crept higher and higher. It sloshed and splashed and spilled until it was all around Mouse's wooden house.

The next morning, Mouse took a swim...

... from INSIDE his bedroom!

"Ssss," said Snake, slithering along the soggy path. "I say, my good man. Don't you know around these parts you have to build your house on stilts?"

"I did not know that," said Mouse.

Mouse found some long poles.

He pounded them into the ground.

He pulled the house up on the stilts.

"There," he said. "Isn't this a fine house?"

That night there was no rain, no thunder, no blowing wind, no rising river.

There was, however, a terrible, loud CRASH.

The next morning, Mouse felt funny...

His ceiling was where his floor should be. "Now what?" said Mouse.
His house was too heavy. It had tipped over.

Mouse stared at his upside-down house.

"Building a house is harder than I thought," he said. Mouse missed his family, too.

Then, he had an idea.

He built a tent around his house. Sawing and sanding and hammering sounds came from the tent. His new friends wondered what he was doing.

Finally Mouse said, "All done." At first, his
friends didn't know what to say.

Suddenly, Frog said, "Burrip! The red tile roof will keep you dry when the rain comes down!"

Turtle said, "Glubbub! And the wood walls will protect you when the wind blows hard!"

Snake said, "Ssss! And the boat will float your house when the river rises. VERY NICE!"

But best of all, Mouse could sail down the river to visit his family. And he did, every Friday.

"What a fine house!" they told him.

Made in the USA
Las Vegas, NV
29 December 2023

83673944R00024